The Little Grumpus
and the TERRIBLE MORNING

Written by
SARA RICHARDS • Illustrated by
TYM STEVENS

Spiral House Publishing
P.O. Box 196
1839 B Ygnacio Valley Road
Walnut Creek, CA, 94598
www.spiralhousepublishing.com
info@spiralhousepublishing.com

ISBN: 978-1-64467-134-4
Made in China

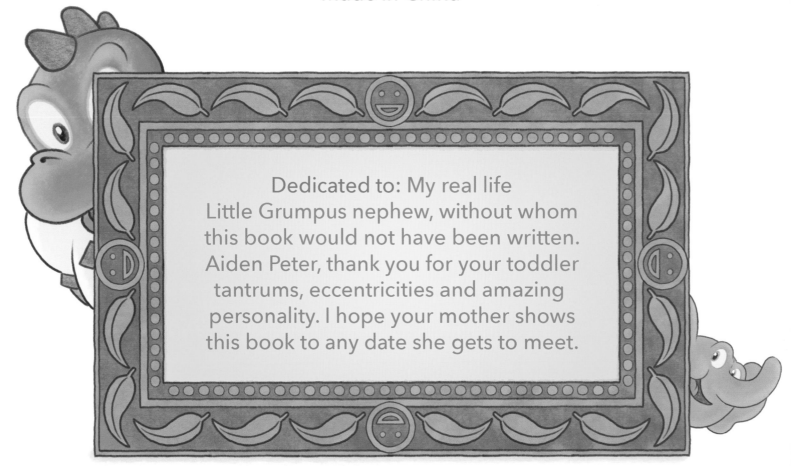

Dedicated to: My real life Little Grumpus nephew, without whom this book would not have been written. Aiden Peter, thank you for your toddler tantrums, eccentricities and amazing personality. I hope your mother shows this book to any date she gets to meet.

"Don't start your day like this again,"
said his favorite stuffed animal, Bo, in warning.

But it was too late...

"Come now, silly!" Mama said, "You have to get up to eat."
But as she lifted up the covers, ice-cold air attacked his feet.

"Too Cold!" yelped Grumpus loudly, curling up into a ball.

He wanted to stay warm in his bed
...maybe he didn't need breakfast after all.

"It's really not that cold," said Bo,
pulling Grumpus' blanket away slightly.

But Grumpus
just scowled down at Bo
and grabbed his blanket
tightly.

Finally, after much debate, Grumpus slithered off the bed and waddled to the kitchen, to await being fed.

"Stop this right now!" said Mama sternly.
"Once you have food, you'll be alright."

And without further warning, she *whisked* him into his chair, his blanket out of sight!

Little Grumpus shivered, cold in the morning air.

"See, this IS a Terrible Morning!" he said,
shooting Bo a glare.

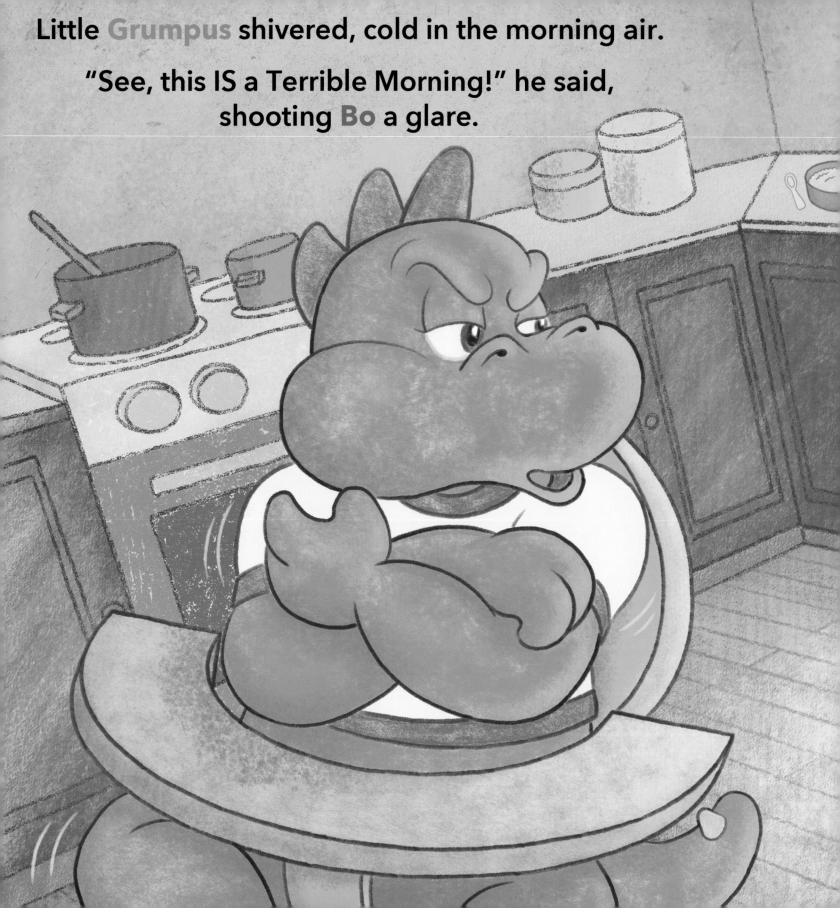

"I didn't see the morning going like this!" said Bo,
from the floor near Grumpus' chair.

"You can't blame this morning on me;
that's simply not fair."

But Grumpus wouldn't listen; he stubbornly kept his frown.

He just *knew* the morning would get worse,
with no good things to be found.

"Here you go," said Mama, setting down Grumpus' food.

"Breakfast will make you warm in no time;
that'll surely brighten your mood!"

"2 Hands, 2 TOOOOOAAAAAASSSTTS!"
cried Grumpus in dismay.

He just HAD to have 2 pieces of toast
for a good start to his day.

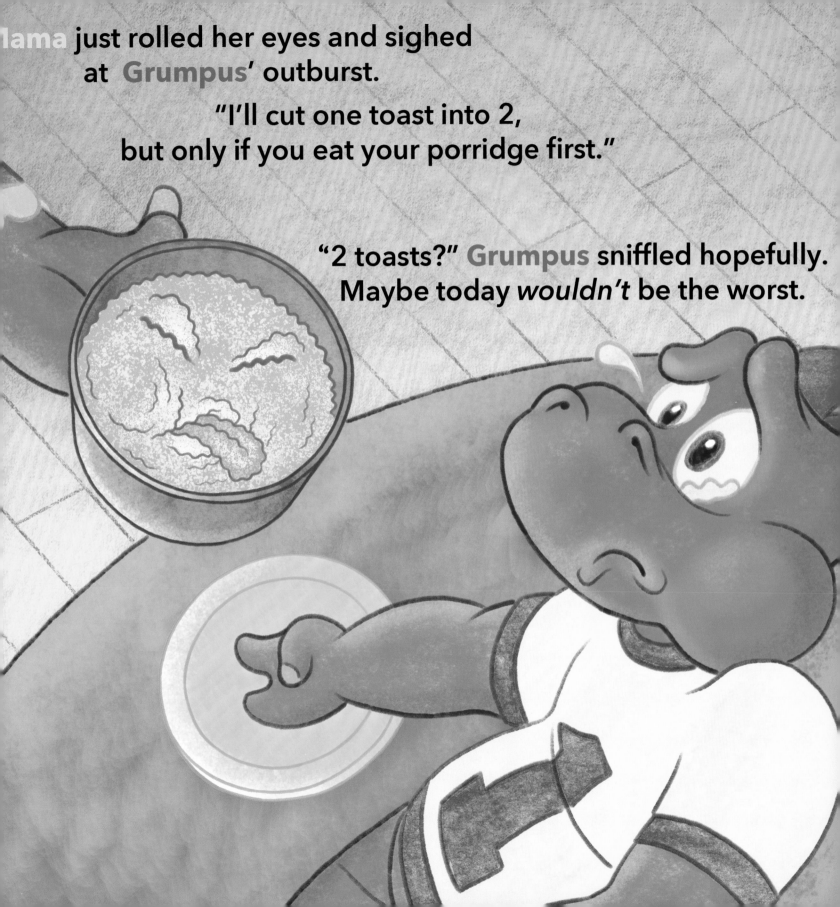

Mama just rolled her eyes and sighed
at Grumpus' outburst.

"I'll cut one toast into 2,
but only if you eat your porridge first."

"2 toasts?" Grumpus sniffled hopefully.
Maybe today *wouldn't* be the worst.

"Or maybe," he thought sneakily, "Mama just needs to see me take ONE bite."

"And once she's brought my toast, I'll just eat that. Then my morning will be alright."

Pleased with his idea,
he ate a spoonful without a fight.

The porridge made his tummy warm,
so he spooned up a second bite.

And another...

...and another...

Until there was no porridge left in sight!

"Want More!" shouted Grumpus, working himself into quite a state.

Standing up in his chair, he grabbed his *new* toast to throw it off his plate.

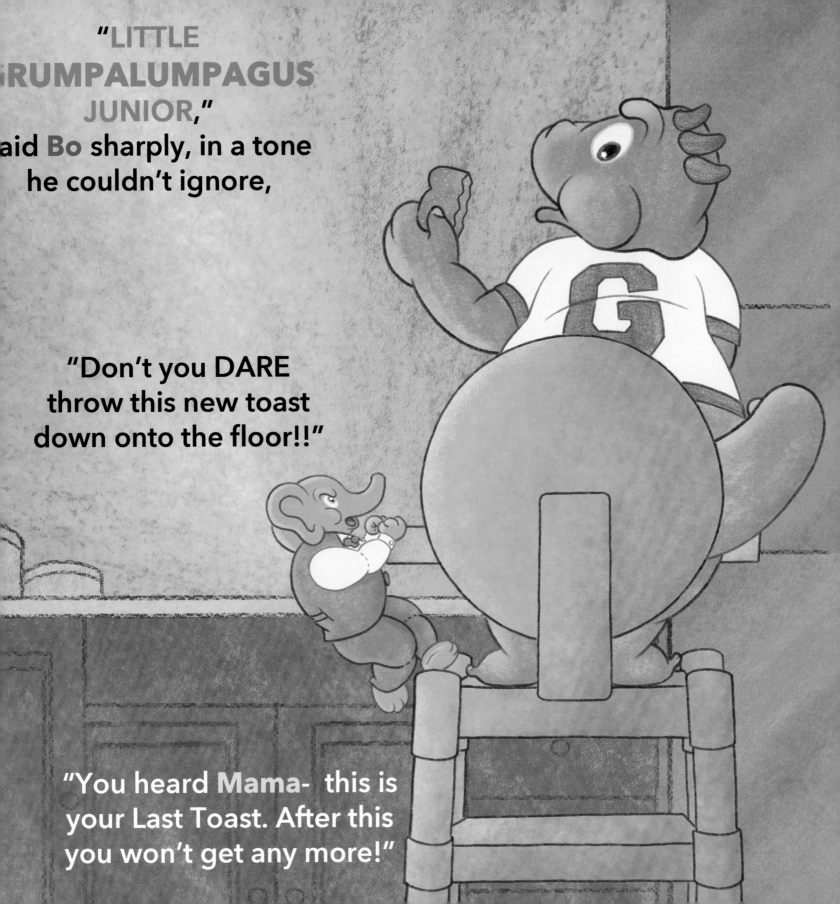

"LITTLE GRUMPALUMPAGUS JUNIOR," said Bo sharply, in a tone he couldn't ignore,

"Don't you DARE throw this new toast down onto the floor!!"

"You heard Mama- this is your Last Toast. After this you won't get any more!"

Little Grumpus paused his
toast-tantrum-throwing plans.

Bo had a point, and he *did* now have
a piece of toast for both his hands...

He nibbled at a toast-corner,
to see if Bo was right.

His eyes widened in surprise-
the toast was a De-light!

And so the Little Grumpus
happily ate...

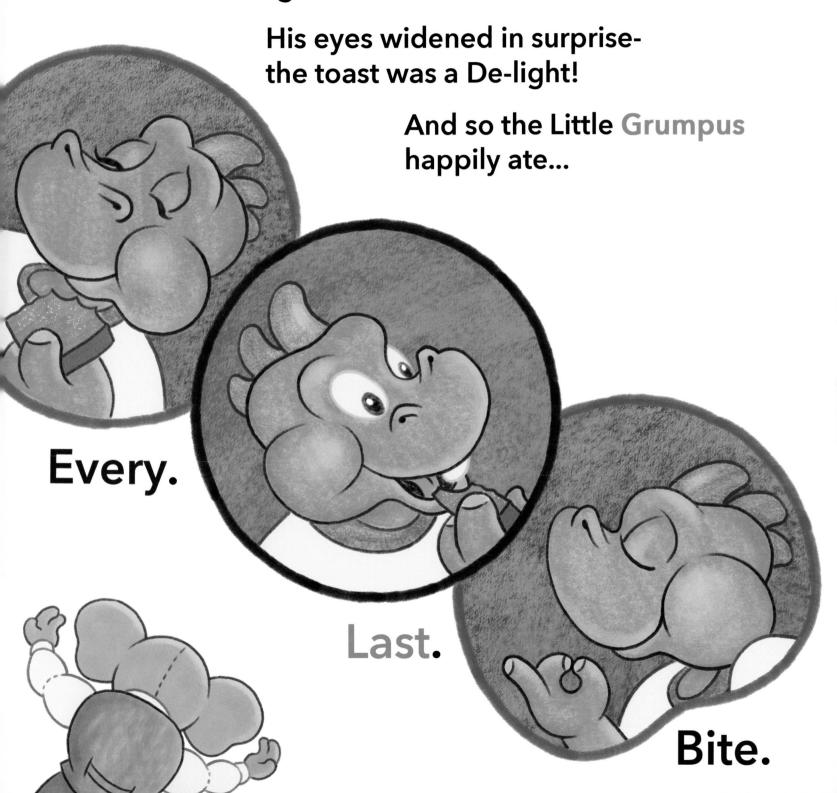

Every.

Last.

Bite.

"Now," said Bo, "wouldn't this morning have been better if you had just stayed positive and calm?"

But Grumpus was too busy eating toast to bother to respond.

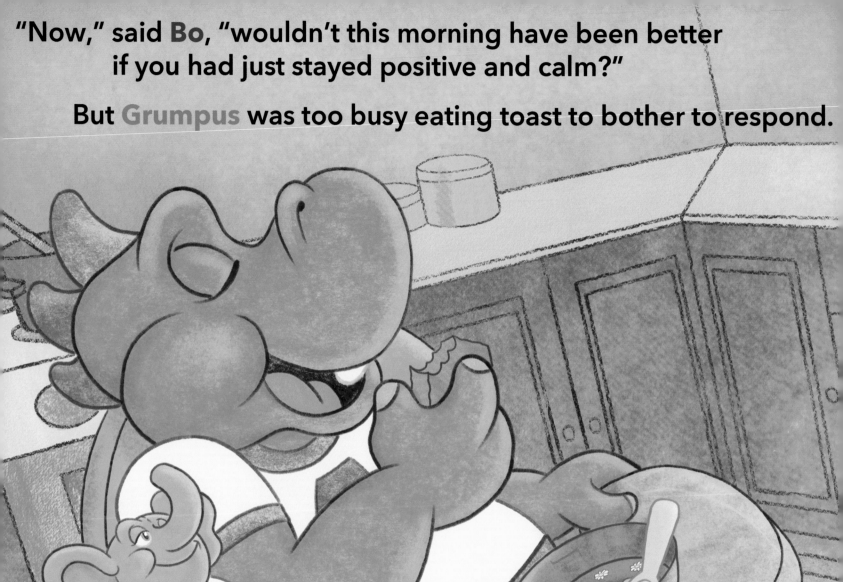

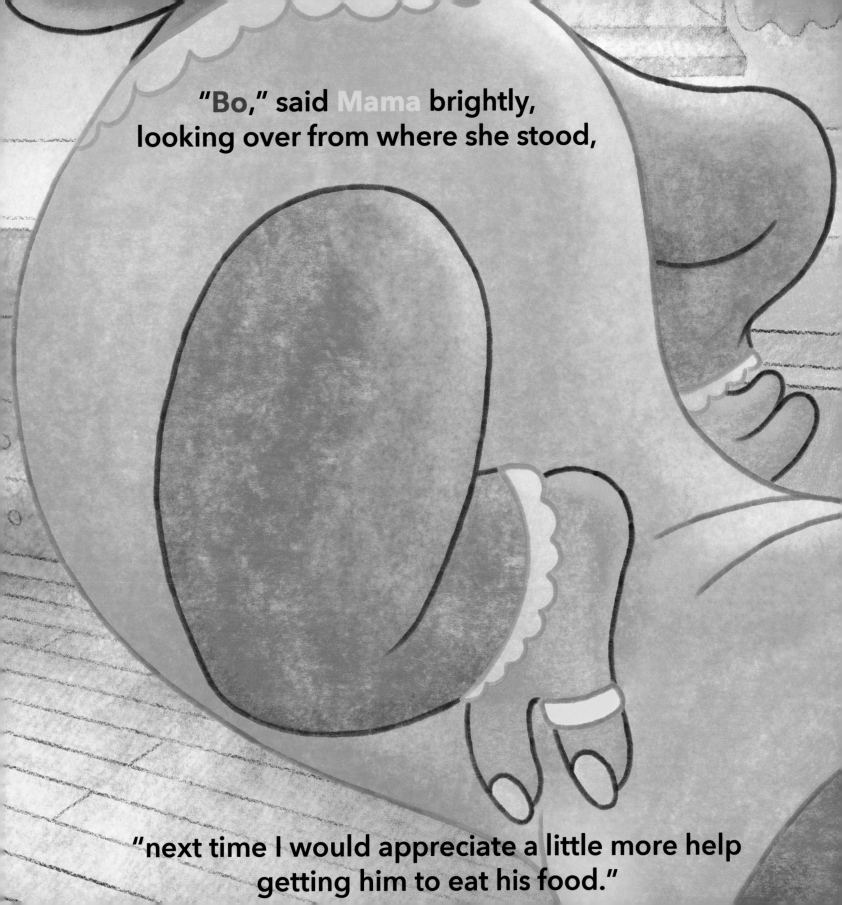

"Bo," said Mama brightly,
looking over from where she stood,

"next time I would appreciate a little more help
getting him to eat his food."

Bo sighed loudly, knowing an argument
with Mama could never be won.

"If there's one thing I learned today," he said,
"it's that an elephant's work is never done."